FIRST FAIRY TALES

Rumpelstiltskin

Margaret Mayo ★ Philip Norman

ORCHARD BOOKS

Once upon a time, there was a foolish farmer who had a beautiful clever daughter.

One day, the farmer went to the palace and started to show off. He said to the king, "I have a beautiful daughter!"

But the king took no notice. So the farmer said, "And she's clever! She can...SPIN STRAW INTO GOLD!"

Now, the king loved gold.
"Oh-ho!" he said. "I'd like to see
your daughter!"

So, the farmer hurried home and told his daughter that the king wanted to see her.

But, when the girl got to the
palace, the king took her to a
room where there was a pile of
straw and a spinning-wheel.

"Spin this straw into gold!" he
said.

And off he went.

The girl didn't know what to
do, and she began to cry...

but then, a strange little man
jumped in through the window.

"Beautiful girl," he said, "why are you crying?"

"I must spin this straw into gold," she answered. "And I don't know how to do it."

"What will you give me," said the little man, "if I do it for you?"

"My necklace," she said. And she gave it to him.

The little man sat down. The
spinning-wheel whirled round and
round, and the straw was spun
into gold.

Then, with a skip and a jump,
he was gone.

When the king saw the gold, he was pleased. But he wanted more. So, he took the girl to a room where there was a bigger pile of straw.

"Spin this straw into gold!" he said.

And off he went.

Again, the girl began to cry…
and then, the strange little man
jumped in through the window.

"More straw!" he said. "What
will you give me if I spin it for
you?"

"My ring," she said. And she
gave it to him.

Again, the spinning-wheel whirled round and round, and the straw was spun into gold. Then, with a skip and a jump, he was gone.

When the king saw the gold, he was very pleased. But he wanted even *more*. So, he took the girl to a room where there was an even bigger pile of straw. It reached right to the ceiling!

"Spin this straw into gold!" he said.

And off he went.

Again, the girl began to cry...
and then, the strange little man
jumped in through the window.

"Even more straw!" he said.
"What will you give me if I spin it
for you?"

"I have nothing left," said the
girl, sadly.

"Then promise," he said, "that when you are queen, you will give me your first little baby."

"Oh!" she said. "All right...I promise."

Once again, the spinning-wheel whirled round and round, and the straw was spun into gold. Then, with a skip and a jump, the little man was gone.

When the king saw the gold, he was very, very pleased. He thought, "This girl is clever and beautiful!"

So, he asked her to marry him, and the farmer's daughter became the queen.

A year passed by, and the queen had a baby. She had forgotten her promise to the little man.

But the little man had not forgotten. One day, he jumped in through the window.

"Now you must give me your baby," he said.

"Oh, no!" she said. "I'll give you jewels…a castle…anything. But not my baby."

"The baby is what I want," he said.

The queen began to cry, and
the little man was sorry for her.

He said, "If you can guess my
name, you can keep your baby. I
will give you three days and three
guesses each day."

As soon as the little man had gone, the queen sent servants all over the land to collect lots of different names.

When the little man came back the next day, she said, "Is your name Caspar? Is it Jehoshaphat? Is it Balthazar?"

But to each one, he said, "No! That's not my name!"

On the second day, the queen said, "Is your name Skinny-legs? Is it Rumble-tummy? Is it Beaky-nose?"

But, to each one, the little man said, "No! That's not my name!"

On the morning of the third day, the queen was worried. She only had three guesses left. Then, one of the servants told her that he had seen a strange little man skipping round a fire in the forest. He was singing this song:

"Around and around,
I dance and I sing,
And nobody knows
I'm Rumpelstiltskin!"

The queen clapped her hands.
"That's his name!" she cried.
"*Rumpelstiltskin!*"

When the little man came for
the last time, the queen said:

"I wonder…is your name…
John?"

"No!" he laughed. "That's not
my name!"

"I wonder…" she said, "could it
be…Tom?"

"No! No!" he laughed. "That's
not my name!"

"Well..." said the queen, "is it...
Rumpelstiltskin?"

"Who told you?" he shouted.
"Who? Who?"

He was so angry, he stamped a
hole in the floor, and whooshed
through it! And he was never seen
again.

Then, the queen picked up her baby, and she gave her lovely baby a great big happy hug!

FIRST FAIRY TALES
by Margaret Mayo
Illustrated by Philip Norman

Enjoy a little more magic with these First Fairy Tales:

❏ Cinderella	1 84121 150 8	£3.99
❏ Hansel and Gretel	1 84121 148 6	£3.99
❏ Jack and the Beanstalk	1 84121 146 X	£3.99
❏ Sleeping Beauty	1 84121 144 3	£3.99
❏ Rumpelstiltskin	1 84121 152 4	£3.99
❏ Snow White	1 84121 154 0	£3.99

Colour Crackers
by Rose Impey
Illustrated by Shoo Rayner

Have you read any Colour Crackers?

❏ A Birthday for Bluebell	1 84121 228 8	£3.99
❏ Hot Dog Harris	1 84121 232 6	£3.99
❏ Tiny Tim	1 84121 240 7	£3.99
❏ Too Many Babies	1 84121 242 3	£3.99

and many other titles.

First Fairy Tales and Colour Crackers are available from all good
bookshops, or can be ordered direct from the publisher:
Orchard Books, PO BOX 29, Douglas IM99 1BQ
Credit card orders please telephone 01624 836000
or fax 01624 837033
or e-mail: bookshop@enterprise.net for details.

To order please quote title, author and ISBN
and your full name and address.
Cheques and postal orders should be
made payable to 'Bookpost plc'.
Postage and packing is FREE within the UK
(overseas customers should add £1.00 per book).

Prices and availability are subject to change.